THE
Island

BRIAN CONTE

PAGE PUBLISHING
Conneaut Lake, PA

First originally published by Page Publishing 2024

ISBN 979-8-89157-526-4 (pbk)
ISBN 979-8-89157-549-3 (digital)

Printed in the United States of America

This story is dedicated to my son, Zeb, who experienced a similar adventure in real life.

DAY 1

We arrived here, and we immediately found a camping site. We're on the small end of the island. We opened some coconuts and ate the meat with our beef stroganoff. There were lots of crabs and lots and lots of ants. I found a young coconut tree I can almost climb. I hope to climb it the next day (using rope). With all our talk of how small the island is, it was surprisingly big. I think we would explore it later today or maybe tomorrow.

DAY 2

Today, we (Dad and I) got up the solar panels, did organization, went around the island, and read the first chapter of *Gödel Escher Bach*. On the trip around the island, we picked up trash. There was an old wives' tale that said when shoes are littered in the water, certain currents favorite either the left or right shoe. This island was a left island. We found six left shoes and only two right shoes.

* * * * *

I woke up in the kayak. I was on a beach. I heard waves behind me.

"Dad?" I called.

No one answered.

* * * * *

Where was I?

I looked around. A jungle was ahead of me. I heard the ocean behind me. The sound of the waves scared me.

A bag was tied to the kayak. This journal was in it. There were daily entries by me. The last one was day 2. What day was it now?

"Dad?" I called again.

I went down the beach. I kept calling for Dad, but there was no response.

I saw something in the sand. It was the journal.

I realized where I was—on another island, alone.

* * * * *

I sat down on the sand. My heart pounded in my chest. My breaths grew short. I buried my head in my hands. I tried to escape the terrifying truth: It seemed I was the only one on this small island.

The kayak was gone when I looked up. The tide must have come in and taken it away while I was walking around the island. That was something Dad had warned me of.

Tears filled my eyes. How could this be happening to me? I was only ten. Until now, I'd never been away from my family. When I was scared, Dad or Mom was always there to help.

Now, I was alone. I had nothing except this journal and the clothes I wore. I had no way to contact anyone, and I couldn't find Dad. I could barely think straight. What was I supposed to do? Who was going to take care of me?

* * * * *

I sat on the beach for a long time, too scared to move. I wouldn't know what to do if I could.

Late in the afternoon, the wind picked up, and I could see black clouds approaching. The waves got bigger and darker and struck a new level of fear in me. I knew I had to get far away from them. I backed up, away from the sea, to the edge of the dark jungle.

The sky got dark and angry. The wind rose and started howling, and the breaking waves lapped at my feet. I didn't have a choice but to go into the jungle.

It was dark there, and cooler than the beach. Coconut trees swayed all around me and their leaves rustling in the wind. Fronds and old coconuts were scattered everywhere on the ground. The undergrowth was so tangled, I almost tripped a few times.

Thump! I jumped at the sound to my left. I stared in that direction but saw nothing. *Thump*! It was louder this time and just to my right. I turned and saw a large coconut rolling toward my feet. Another coconut fell a few feet from me. *Thump!*

I looked up. The palm trees, as tall as telephone poles, were swinging wildly in the wind. Each had a cluster of basketball-sized coconuts at the top, ready to drop onto me.

I started to run. *Thump. Thump. Thump-thump*. Coconuts rained from the trees. I knew it would hurt if one hit me. I stumbled through the dark jungle. Thorns scratched my body. Trees tried to get in my way. The coconuts kept falling around me.

The jungle got denser and darker, but I kept going. It got completely dark, and I couldn't see anything, just feel the trees as they slammed into me. I got turned around and lost my sense of direc-

6

tion. For all I knew, I was going in circles, but I kept running. I had no idea what I was looking for. I only knew I had to get away from the ocean and away from the trees and falling coconuts.

Suddenly, I stepped into a bright clearing; a circle of light carved from the dark jungle. The air was completely still and quiet. The jungle stopped abruptly at the edge of the clearing, as if held back by magic. No coconuts fell here. Scratched, bruised, and out of breath, I bent over and gulped mouthfuls of fresh air. Then I looked up.

In the center of the clearing stood an enormous tree, towering above the jungle, glowing in the fading sunlight. I looked at it in awe. The tree was different from any I'd seen on the island. It wasn't a palm tree. It looked like the trees we had back home. It was enormous – easily twice as tall as the surrounding trees. It was as thick as a refrigerator. It stood straight and strong, while the palm trees bent and swayed. The bark was as smooth as skin. Huge branches stuck out from the trunk at right angles. A network of roots spread from its base and formed a crisscross pattern on the ground.

As soon as my eyes fell on the tree, I felt a sense of relief, of safety, of comfort. I ran to the tree, and two of its large roots embraced me. For the first time since I'd arrived on this island, I felt safe and protected. I took some deep breaths and leaned against the tree's warm trunk.

In the fading light, I wrote these journal entries for today. Writing down my thoughts helped comfort me. It wasn't long before I fell asleep.

* * * * *

My sleep was filled with a terrifying nightmare.

I was alone in the kayak, at night, in the middle of a violent storm. Huge dark waves surrounded me. Wind screamed and tore at my soaked clothes. Freezing rain pelted me. Lightning flashes revealed angry massive waves as far as I could see.

The waves tossed me up and down like a cork in a whirlpool. They crashed across the kayak, soaking me. All I could do was hang on as tightly as I could.

I'd never been so afraid.

"DAD!" I screamed into the shrieking wind. "DAD!"

* * * * *

I awoke bathed in warm sunlight. The jungle was calm now. The sky was a brilliant blue, with no clouds in sight. I could hear the gentle surf far away through the jungle.

My nightmare was fading, but it still filled me with fear and loneliness. Like in the dream, I was alone, and I didn't know where Dad was. I had never been in this situation before, and it terrified me. I knew I had to be brave, but I just couldn't.

I felt the comforting warmth of the tree all around me. The roots had moved close against me and embraced me in a warm hug. I felt comforted from my nightmares, safe in the embrace of the tree.

But I was also hungry and very thirsty. I felt a gnawing in my stomach, and my throat was dry. I knew I hadn't had anything to eat or drink since arriving on the island, and who knew for how long before that?

I had to find something to eat and drink—but where? I had seen nothing but sand, trees, and dirt since I've been on the island—nothing edible. There was no fresh water in sight, and I hadn't encountered any pools of water or streams when I walked around the island yesterday. I didn't know where to start.

So I just sat there. Someone, somehow, would help me—just as they always had. I knew it didn't make sense, but I didn't know what else to do. I tried not to think about the fact that neither Mom nor Dad was here.

While I waited for someone to help, I looked around me, and a green grass-like plant carpeted the clearing, broken up by the tree's roots. There was nothing on it, up to the edge of the jungle.

There were some odd-shaped sticks at the base of the tree. I picked one up. It looked like a man, with offshoots for arms and legs. The other sticks were similar. They were the size of my Bionicles at home. *Well,* I thought, *at least I could play with these while I waited.*

I played for most of the day, acting out all kinds of imaginary battles and adventures, waiting for someone to come help me. I got thirstier and thirstier as the day wore on. I did my best to not think about the reality of my situation.

By evening, my thirst was getting unbearable. My stomach ached. My lips were hard and dry and painful. I felt lightheaded and dizzy. I leaned back against the tree, tired and defeated.

That's when I saw it. Two of the roots were cupped as if they were hands and filled with water. My heart leapt. I crawled over, and I reached out and touched it. It was clear and wet to the touch.

There was water just a few feet from where I had been playing all day. Eagerly, I scooped some up with my cupped hands and took a few tentative sips. It tasted good, cool, and delicious. It eased my dry throat, and I started to feel better.

I couldn't figure out how I had missed it earlier or how it had gotten there. I had looked everywhere in the clearing. I couldn't explain it. But I didn't think too much about it—it was just what I needed.

I drank until I thought my stomach would burst. No matter how much I drank, the pool of water didn't get any smaller. When I finally could drink no more, I returned to the tree and rested against it. I felt a lot better. It wasn't long before I drifted to sleep.

* * * * *

That night, I had another nightmare.

I was drifting in the kayak in the heart of a terrifying storm. The freezing cold and howling winds stabbed me like knives. My fingers were so numb, I could barely grip the sides of the kayak.

But this time, I sensed Dad in the kayak behind me. He was grunting from the strain of paddling against the wind and waves.

I knew Dad needed my help paddling, but I was frozen with fear. I held on to the kayak as tightly as I could. Dad struggled behind me, and he sounded exhausted. The kayak rose and fell violently, one second suspended in the air and the next plunging into the water.

A gigantic wave came from the left and hit us like a wall. Before I knew it, I was underwater. Shocked and disoriented, I kicked frantically, but I couldn't find which way was up. I choked on salt water and panicked. A moment later, my head shot up above the water. The kayak was right next to me, but I had no way to get back in or even to hold on to it.

I felt Dad grab me from behind and, with one strong thrust, push me over the side of the kayak. I fell to the bottom, shivering and coughing.

When I was able to sit up, a lightning flash revealed Dad a few feet from the kayak, swimming hard toward it. Another lightning flash and he was further away, still swimming toward the kayak. Another flash and he was even further away. He didn't seem to be swimming anymore.

That was the last time I saw Dad.

* * * *

I woke again to the warm embrace of the roots. My nightmare slowly dissolved and was replaced by my surroundings, the warm tree, the bright morning light, and the clearing.

Something moved at my feet. It was a baby bird, with a white chest, blue wings, and a large beak. It walked clumsily around my feet, looking at me with curiosity. I had read about the local birds before coming, and I recognized it—a kingfisher. It was a baby, and it looked like it couldn't fly yet—it must have fallen out of its nest. I looked up but couldn't find a nest, and I looked around, but there were no other birds in sight. Where had it come from? Where were its parents? I picked it up. It trembled in my hands. *It must be terrified to be young and alone,* I thought.

It was a beautiful bird, with sharp black eyes. Its feet had a claw facing backward, like a talon. I wondered if it was thirsty. I carried it to the pool of water. It took a sip hesitantly and then took several long sips.

I watched it drink. "Are you lost too?" I asked. I knew it was just a bird, but it was the first creature I'd seen since being on the island. I felt a bond with it. "I think I'll call you Taly," I said, thinking of its talons.

It was a relief to have someone to be with, even if it was just a bird. I really wasn't used to being alone for so long, but while Taly brought me some relief, I felt some responsibility to it. I picked it up again and cupped him gently in my hands, feeling its warmth and fluttering heartbeat.

* * * * *

Holding Taly calmed me and made me feel like I wasn't alone. I could have held him all day. But by afternoon, my hunger was a sharp and constant pain in my stomach that I couldn't ignore. I knew I had to find something to eat.

Just inside the jungle on the ground, I saw coconuts. Coconuts—I remembered the first day we were on Enedrik. Dad had opened a coconut with an axe, and there was edible white meat inside. But I didn't have an axe. I needed another way to open them.

I looked closely at one. The husk was brown and hard. I pressed my thumbnail against it, making a small mark. There wasn't any obvious way to crack open the husk to get to the nut inside. I picked it up and threw it to the ground, but nothing happened. I tried stomping on it. Like a basketball, it flexed a bit under my weight, but didn't break. I tried hitting it against a root. A small dent appeared on the outside of the coconut.

I hit the coconut against the root again and again with all my strength. I made more dents, but the husk showed no signs of opening. I tried another coconut and another, but the result was always the same. I couldn't do more than dent the husks.

The coconuts were heavy, and the work was exhausting. I had to take frequent breaks, and by late afternoon, I could try no more. I gave up. I sat down on a tree root, exhausted and beaten, the ground littered with dented coconuts around me. The hopefulness I had yesterday after drinking the water was rapidly disappearing.

Taly sat next to me. He seemed hungry too.

I racked my brain. What could I eat? I wished Dad were here. He'd know what to do.

I cuddled with Taly against the trunk and drifted off to sleep. In my dream, Dad opened all the coconuts with an axe. We shared the meat, which was delicious. He was smiling and talking. I held Taly in my hands. I felt happy.

* * * * *

Crack! I woke up with my heart pounding. It was still dark. All I could hear was loud, sharp cracking all around me. I felt Taly move and held him close. The cracking must have scared him too.

We were on a stout tree branch that held us a few feet from the ground. I don't remember climbing up here—in fact, I don't remember seeing this branch yesterday.

Suddenly, a crab sidestepped into the moonlight below me. I froze. This wasn't like any other crab I had ever seen. It was gigantic, as big as a small dog. In the moonlight, its shell looked dark orange or brown. A coconut crab, I remembered from my reading. Its pincers could crush bones, and one of its favorite foods was birds.

Another crab appeared below us and then another, and then a bunch came into view like a wave. They picked up the coconuts I had left on the ground, cracking open each in turn and eating the meat inside.

I was petrified. I backed up against the tree, my eyes darting everywhere. Taly was awake and trembling again. I held him close against my chest. I knew he was scared too. I stroked his head.

"It's okay," I whispered, not believing it myself.

After a while, the crabs finally moved on, back into the jungle, leaving the clearing strewn with coconut shell pieces. It was quiet now, but what if they came back? Did they come this way every night? I didn't dare go back to the ground. I lay face down on the branch and hugged it, wide awake.

* * * * *

When I finally fell asleep, my nightmares returned.

This dream started out differently. It was morning, sunny and warm, and I was having breakfast on Enedrik with Dad. We were talking about what might make left shoes drift differently than right ones and our plans for the day. Dad wanted to explore the island next to us—an island we could see from Enedrik, maybe a mile away. I packed my journal and pens into the waterproof dry bag in the kayak, and we set out.

The trip across the channel to the island went smoothly. There was a current between the islands, but we stayed on track. After paddling for an hour, we arrived at the other island. We pulled the kayak up on the beach—Dad pulled it up extra. "Because of the tide," he said, and then we set off to explore the island. We picked our way carefully around the shore, across beaches and over rocks. The island was about the size of Enedrik and similar in many ways.

About halfway around, I saw Dad look out across the water at some clouds. "Looks like a storm is coming," he said. "We better head back to Enedrik."

By the time we got back to the kayak and pushed off, the clouds were closer and darker. Shortly after we pushed off, I felt a few drops of rain. It looked like the storm might hit us before we got back. We paddled hard.

The storm reached us in the middle of the channel. The winds were strong and pushed our kayak off course, toward the open water. We kept turning back to Enedrik, and we paddled harder.

The heavy rain started, and the wind picked up more. The waves rose and were capped with white now. The wind was strong enough now that we struggled to stay on course. A scary pit was growing in my stomach.

Dad yelled something to me, but I couldn't hear him over the increasing roar of the wind. We were paddling as hard as we could toward Enedrik, but it seemed to be getting further away. Now I could see it only when the waves picked the kayak up high. After a few minutes, I couldn't even see it then.

I could hear Dad grunting and paddling as hard as he could, but to no avail. We were on the open sea now, in the middle of a storm, with no land in sight, just us, the kayak, and the increasingly angry ocean.

* * * * *

I know what day it is now. It's day 7. My memory had returned.
Day 3 was the day I couldn't remember at first, when Dad and I
paddled the kayak to the neighboring island and then got caught in
a storm on our way back. That's the day I last saw Dad. That night,
I was carried on the storm to this island. Day 4 was when I woke up
on this island. On day 5, I found water, and on day 6, I tried to open
the coconuts and saw the crabs at night. Today was day 7.

That meant it had been four days since I had seen Dad. I hadn't
been apart from my parents that long, ever. I needed them more than
ever. How could I do this alone? Where was Dad? I wondered. When
would I see him again?

I looked around. The ground was littered with pieces of coconut shells from last night. I eagerly inspected the shell pieces, but the
crabs had picked all of them clean.

The pool of water was still there. I took a long drink. Taly did
the same. The water helped, but there was still a growing pain in my
stomach. I hadn't eaten now in three days. I needed food.

Maybe there is food in the jungle? I thought. But I didn't dare go
back in the jungle. It was dark and scary, and the only thing I knew
for sure that was in there were the falling coconuts and the crabs. The
clearing was warm and bright and free of falling coconuts, and I felt
a sense of safety around the tree, which had provided a haven from
the crabs last night.

I played with my stick toys for most of the day. I kept waiting
for an adult to come help me, though deep in my heart, I was starting
to doubt they would. The pain in my stomach only grew.

I reached a point when I could play no more. Nor could I come to terms with my reality. It was too overwhelming. My heart beat fast. I could feel the beginnings of a panic attack. I was more upset than I had been in a while, maybe ever. My heart ached for something familiar and comforting.

I noticed the corner of some papers at the base of the tree, covered in dirt. I picked them up, brushed off the dirt, and started reading.

"Walking back to camp through the swamp, Sam wondered whether to tell his father what he had seen."

It was the beginning of one of my favorite books, *The Trumpet of the Swan*! It looked like the whole first chapter was there. I had no idea how the pages got there. But it was just what I needed to comfort me. As I read, I could feel my heart rate slowing and the panic dissipating. By the end of the chapter, I felt much better.

That night, I dreamed about Sam, watching the trumpeter swans in their nest in the swamp. Sam had led his dad to the nest, but when he arrived and looked around, his dad was gone. Sam called out for him, but there was no response, and so Sam waited, for hours and days and weeks.

* * * * *

Dad isn't coming.

Deep down inside, I already knew. But this morning, I admitted it to myself for the first time.

I had no idea what happened to him after the storm. Maybe he made it back to Enedrik. Maybe he washed up on another island. Maybe he was still adrift at sea. But I knew he would have come for me by now if he could. That he hadn't meant that he couldn't.

And I knew Mom wouldn't come. She wasn't expecting us home for another two weeks, and even if she came to the islands, she wouldn't expect me to be off Enedrik and, if she did, would have no idea which of the thousands of islands I was on.

There was a huge hole inside me, as if part of me was missing. I'd felt like this since I arrived on the island, but I ignored it and hoped the feeling would subside. Now, it gnawed at me almost as badly as my hunger.

I was on my own now. I needed to figure out how to survive by myself. I needed to be brave. How would I manage alone on an uninhabited island? I was afraid to leave the clearing, but there was no food here. I checked for the pool of water, but it and the roots holding it were gone.

I played with my toys, but I even stopped doing that in the afternoon, too hungry to continue. Taly had his eyes closed now, and he looked very weak.

That night, I dreamed about my family. I was at the dinner table with Dad, Mom, and my sisters, Celeste and Calista. We were having pasta. It was the best pasta I had ever eaten—every bite was indescribably delicious. I ate and ate, and we never ran out. My sisters seemed so real next to me. But when I reached out to them, they and the food vanished. I was left in the dark, hungry, and all alone.

* * * * *

I woke up feeling sad and scared. I felt like I wanted to cry. My stomach ached for food. My heart ached to not be alone, and I knew now that my parents were not coming to save me. I just lay there under the tree, too weak and sad to do anything. "I give up," I told myself. I couldn't survive without someone to help.

And that's when I saw them.

Eyes.

At first glance, they seemed to float from a branch above me. It took a moment to realize that the face of a boy was looking at me.

My mind had a hard time processing what I was seeing. All I could do was stare. Was he real, or was I dreaming? Who was he? Had he been here all this time?

* * * * *

The boy and I stared at each other. Then he climbed down to the ground. He looked around my age, maybe a bit older. He was taller and more muscular. He had long dark hair and tanned skin. He wore only faded shorts and a necklace that looked like it was made from a stick. He seemed relaxed and confident.

I couldn't believe he was here. Just a few minutes ago, I felt so hopeless—hungry, thirsty, and alone. Now, everything had changed. I have a human companion on the island. Maybe he could help me find food and water and help me and Taly survive. I felt new hope.

Without a word, the boy started looking at the remaining dented coconuts scattered on the ground. He picked one up and examined it closely. Then he walked to the edge of the clearing. He stepped into the jungle. He turned around, waiting for me to follow.

It was something I couldn't do on my own, but the boy gave me new courage. I followed him into the jungle, where it was dark and cool.

We had only gone about twenty feet when the boy stopped. He pointed with his toe at a large rock protruding from the ground and handed the coconut to me.

Oh, I thought, looking at the rock. It was dark gray and poked above the ground. *Hmm,* I thought. I hadn't been able to break the coconut's husk against the root, but the rock was harder and pointed. Maybe that would work better.

I knelt next to the rock. I lifted the coconut above my head and then slammed it into the rock. A small gash appeared in the husk. I did it again, and the gash got bigger. I did it a few more times, and

22

the gash was now the size of my hand, and I could see the light-colored fibrous materials inside.

I grabbed the edge of the husk and pulled with all my might. A piece of the husk came off in my hands. Bit by bit, I was able to completely remove the husk and then strip the fibers inside from the nut.

The nut was brown and hard, and I could hear liquid inside. Now, the challenge was how to get it. If I smashed the nut open, the liquid would spill on the ground.

The boy pointed to three spots on one side of the nut that were dark brown. He handed me a twig and pointed at one of the spots.

I pressed the end of the twig on one of the spots, hard. With some effort, I was able to poke it through. I raised the nut to my lips and drank the cool liquid inside.

The coconut water felt so good going down my parched throat, and I felt better right away.

When I was done, I smashed the nut on the rock. It broke into several pieces, each with white coconut meat inside. Eagerly, I ate the meat. The pain in my stomach lessened with each bite.

I couldn't believe how much better I felt. Earlier, I was ready to give up. Now, just a few hours later, with the help of the boy and by being brave enough to follow him into the jungle, I had found food, water, and a new friend. And now that I knew how to open a coconut, with all the coconuts on the island, feeling hungry or thirsty wasn't going to be a problem anymore.

I felt very different. I'd reached a turning point. It changed everything. I wasn't scared anymore. I felt a sense of pride and hope.

I had learned an important lesson: A little bravery can make the difference between life and death. I would need to be brave to survive.

* * * * *

I kept opening coconuts until I couldn't eat or drink anymore. Not all of them were good—some didn't have water in them, or the meat was dry or spoiled.

After a while, I learned to tell which coconuts were good by how young they looked on the outside, how heavy they were, and if I heard liquid sloshing inside when I shook them. I was so happy, I wanted to thank the boy, but he was gone. I'd been so focused on the coconuts I never noticed him leave.

I took one of the pieces and a whole nut and started back to the clearing. When I got back to Taly, he drank the water that I poured in my hand but wouldn't touch the coconut meat. *Of course*, I thought, *he is a carnivore*. I would have to find him meat.

That night, I dreamed of the boy. He was my older brother, and we were always together. We lived together, went to school together, and played together. He showed me how to do many things, and I felt confident and safe around him.

* * * * *

When I woke up, my clothes and the ground around me were wet. It had rained overnight. I should make some kind of shelter, something to protect me from the rain and sun. I got a bunch of palm fronds from the edge of the clearing, took them to the tree, and made a little lean-to by leaning the fronds against the tree.

I was worried about Taly. He hadn't eaten since I first found him. I told him I'd look for food, before putting him back on the branch.

I went back into the jungle, this time venturing past the rock. I searched all over the jungle but didn't see any animals that could be a source of meat for Taly. I sat down and thought.

If Dad were here, I know he'd encourage me to think outside the box. *If there was no food on the island, maybe there was food off it, like fish,* I thought. Maybe I could catch a fish for Taly.

I had no idea how to do that. I knew fishermen used a fishing line, hook, and bait, but I only had bait—the coconut meat. The only thing I could think of was to sprinkle the meat on the water and then try to grab the fish when they came for it. Deep down, I knew this was very unlikely, but I couldn't think of anything else.

I headed to the beach, taking the coconut meat that Taly had not eaten. It was scary to go back to the sea, but I knew I had to be brave. I walked through the jungle to the beach and then down to the edge of the sea.

As soon as I saw the breaking waves, I knew this wouldn't work. The bait would scatter immediately, and I wouldn't be able to see the fish through the breaking waves in any event. I had to get past the waves, but there was no way I was walking into the ocean, even with my newfound bravery, and in any event, the water was probably too deep out there.

I started walking around the island, hoping to find a place where the water was calmer. Midway, I came to a place where a palm tree had fallen into the water. It hadn't been there when I first walked around the island—it must have fallen down in the storm.

The tree stretched over the waves to where the water was calm. Maybe out there, my idea would work.

The thought of crawling out on the tree, inches from the dark water, was terrifying. Walking next to the sea was one thing, but crawling out over it on a tree trunk was something else altogether.

But I had to be brave. Taly needed food, and this was the only way I could figure out how to get him some.

I wrapped my arms around the tree. Inch by inch, I crawled out on the fallen tree. Once I was halfway out on the tree, the ocean below me became stiller, and by its color, I could tell it was deeper. I stopped, threw in a few coconut meat crumbs, and waited.

After a few minutes, I caught some movement below the surface, and a fish grabbed one of the crumbs. I tried to grab it, but the fish was gone as soon as I moved a muscle. It darted away, and all I accomplished was splashing myself with water.

I tried a few more times. I tried waiting with my hand hovering just over the surface, in order to grab the fish more quickly. But it was hopeless. The fish were just too fast. There was no way I was going to catch one this way.

I gave up and crawled back to shore. I was feeling frustrated and hopeless again. I didn't know how I was going to feed Taly.

When I got to the shore, I saw the boy sitting at the edge of the jungle. He had been watching me. He turned around and started walking into the jungle. I followed him.

He went to a bamboo grove I passed earlier, pointed to a short stalk, and made a motion to pull it. I pulled it hard, and it broke off at the base. It left a sharp point where it broke.

He went back to the fallen palm tree and I followed him. He seemed to have a plan. He acted where I tended to worry and get scared. I admired that.

He took some of the coconut meat, and holding the bamboo stalk, he walked along the tree trunk like a cat, confident and seemingly without fear. *He was so brave,* I thought. I wish I could be that brave.

When he got to the spot where I had been, he dropped a crumb in the water. He held the tip of the bamboo stalk like a spear a couple of inches above the floating crumb.

He didn't move for several minutes. Then a fish flipped at the end of the spear before I even saw the spear move or heard the splash. It happened so quickly it seemed like an instant.

The boy walked toward me. The fish was still twisting and gasping on the spear. It was a silver fish as large as my foot. Its wet scales looked like mirrors in the sunlight. Within a few seconds, it stopped moving. The boy removed it from the spear and set it down. He handed me the spear. He wanted me to try.

I took a deep breath and approached the tree. Slowly and carefully, I walked down the trunk the way the boy did. He made it look easy, but all I could think about was the water beneath me. I stared at my feet and shuffled slowly out on the log.

When I came to the spot where the boy caught the fish, I broke off a crumb of coconut meat and dropped it in the water. I tried to keep still and raised the spear. I thought about what I'd do when I saw the fish, how I'd react, and where to aim.

Within a few minutes, several fish swam by. They were too far for me to reach, so I waited.

A couple of minutes later, a larger silver fish darted right below me. I thrust my spear at it, but it was gone before the tip of my spear hit the water. The fish was far too fast. This wasn't going to be as easy as the boy made it look.

I raised my spear and brought the tip closer to the water. I tensed up and got ready to strike. Another larger fish swam close. I thrust again. I missed again. Another fish swam by and another. Each time, they were gone before my spear hit the water.

I thought about my challenge. If I was going to spear a fish, I'd have to react faster than the fish. But how could I do that? It seemed impossible. The fish acted on reflex, so how could I react faster? Then

27

it came to me. If I was going to catch a fish, I'd have to think like one, which meant not thinking at all.

I took a deep breath and narrowed my focus to the spot of water under the crumb. I cleared my thoughts of everything—my situation, my fears, and my concern for Taly—and focused on the spot. It was hard to clear my mind, but if I was going to survive, I had no choice.

I imagined myself as one big arm muscle, tense and ready to strike the instant I saw a flash of fish. There would be nothing but the flash and the strike, flash and strike, flash strike, strike flash. They would be one and the same. There would be no thought process between them. The flash was the strike and vice versa. One could not happen without the other. They were physically linked.

I was struggling to hang onto the flipping fish before I realized what just happened. I remembered the strike and the flash as one. I lifted the flipping fish out of the water. I did it! I outfished a fish. I beamed with pride.

This fish was a good size. It was about as long as my forearm, blue with black stripes. It gasped at the end of my spear, still trying to free itself. By the time I brought it back to the beach, it wasn't moving.

I brought the fish to Taly and fed it to him. He had no problem with the raw meat, but when I tried it, I almost gagged. I was hungry, but the meat was slimy and tasted terrible. I'd have to cook it. I wished I had a fire, but for now, I was happy. Taly and I both had food.

* * * * *

For the first time since I arrived at the island, I stayed awake past sunset. Without the moonlight, it got dark quickly. It was more than darkness, though. It was like a black wall I couldn't see through. When I arrived, the moon was waning, so I had a little light. But now, it was just pitch black.

It scared me. How would I know if the crabs came? But then, something amazing happened. The first star appeared in the sky. It was bright like a flashlight shining in the dark. Seeing it chased away my fear. The more I watched the sky, the more stars appeared, twinkling like a Christmas tree.

After my eyes adjusted to the dark, I noticed a faint blue glow through the trees that seemed to come from the beach. I got up and slowly walked through the jungle, staring in the dim blue light to make sure there was no movement around me. The closer I got to the beach, the brighter the glow became.

When I got to the beach, I could see that the blue glow came from the waves crashing onto the beach. The entire beach glowed a deep blue as far as I could see. Along with the glittering stars, it was the most beautiful thing I'd ever seen.

I sat in the sand and watched the water for a long time. Then I thought of something. Right next to me in the sand was an old bottle. I filled the bottle with the blue water. It lit my way back to the tree like a lantern. It dimmed after a while, but I found I could just shake the bottle to light it up again.

I had light! Not only did I feel safer walking around, but now, I could write in my journal at night by the glow of the bottle.

* * * * *

The giant crabs came back last night. I woke up to several sharp cracks. The noise was so loud, it sounded like the crabs were just outside the shelter. I grabbed Taly and pressed myself against the tree. The crabs shuffled around, and I saw movement through the gaps in the shelter.

What would happen if they got any closer? Would they attack me? The shelter couldn't protect me. I could try and run away, but how far would I get in the dark jungle? I was safer by the tree. At least I could watch them and get away if I needed to.

But the crabs never got any closer. They scuttled and cracked for a long time before they finally disappeared. I couldn't sleep after that, so I stayed awake for a long time, until finally my eyes got heavy and I drifted off to sleep.

In the morning, I noticed that my pile of coconuts was gone. All that was left were scattered pieces of coconut shell. The crabs must have eaten all the meat. Lesson learned: Don't stockpile coconuts in the open.

* * * * *

I didn't see the boy when I woke up, but later, I noticed him sitting on a branch above me. He watched me but made no effort to climb down.

I couldn't figure out how he got up there. The branch was at least ten feet high, and there were no lower branches to climb on. I walked around the tree and checked the trunk. Then I noticed several stubby bumps or holes in the bark that he must have used as hand or footholds.

I reached for the bump above my head and stepped into a hole in the trunk a couple of feet high. I carefully pulled myself up. I remembered seeing some kids at a rock climbing park, so I knew I had to coordinate my hands and feet. Little by little, I climbed until I reached the branch where the boy sat. I pulled myself over and sat beside him.

There was another branch at this height so close behind us, I could almost lean back on it. I wondered if I could sleep here instead of the shelter, but there was no way I could keep myself from falling off.

I glanced down and saw Taly looking at us. He probably thought it was funny to see me in the tree while he was on the ground. He spread his wings and folded them back against his body. He was looking better every day.

The boy got up and took a step out on the branch. In a single motion, he leaned down, grabbed the branch, jumped backward, and swung around. He dangled from the branch and then let go and landed on the ground like a cat. It looked so easy. I could tell by the way he looked at me that he wanted me to try it.

I briefly considered it, but there was no way. I carefully climbed down the tree using the same hand and footholds. It was harder climbing down. My foot slipped from the last foothold, and I fell the last couple of feet. I picked myself up and looked toward the boy.

The boy was now walking toward the jungle. I followed him back to the bamboo grove. This time, the boy snapped off a dozen tall stalks and broke them into four and five-foot sections. He bundled them up and gave them to me to carry. He also pulled off some vines from a nearby tree.

When we got back to the tree, the boy tied up my bundle of bamboo with the vine. Taking the other end with him, he climbed up to the first branch and used the vine to pull up the bamboo. I followed him up the tree.

Once in the tree, he placed the bundle of bamboo across both branches near the base. He took one stalk and tied a vine to each end. Then he laid the stalk across the two branches, placed a second stalk beside it, and looped the vines around the bottom of the branches and over the two stalks. He added another stalk beside the first two and repeated the process. Then he gave me the vine so I could do the same to the rest of the stalks. It was like we were sewing them to the tree branches. When I was done, he tied the vines tightly to the last stalk.

We built a platform across the two branches big enough to lie down on. Two other branches had moved to just above each edge of the platform, forming a simple railing. I lay down on the platform, and it felt sturdy. It may not have felt like my bed at home, but it was a safe place to sleep away from the crabs and anything else lurking in the darkness.

* * * * *

When we climbed down from the treehouse, the boy picked up some palm fronds from the shelter. He put them stem first into one of the wide-mouth bottles I found. I didn't understand what he was doing at first, but then I figured it out. It was a rainwater collection system. The next time it rained, the fronds would collect the water in the bottle—smart!

The boy then took me back into the jungle, near the bamboo grove, and pointed up. I saw several large fruits growing from the trees above me. They were as big as large melons and had bumpy green skin. I didn't see how I could reach them, but it was good to know they were there.

The boy then took me further into the jungle and pointed up toward bunches of yellow bananas just above my head. I couldn't believe how I missed them all the times I'd come this way. These were within my reach, so I plucked a big banana from the closest bunch. I peeled it and bit into it. It was a little unripe, but it was a welcome change from coconut meat. I pulled off more from the bunch and brought them back to the tree.

When I got back, I smelled what was left of the fish we ate yesterday. It smelled awful. Flies swarmed around it, and even Taly wouldn't touch it. I wrapped it up in some leaves, took it to the beach, and tossed it in the water. It was too hot to keep fish for long, so I'd have to catch a fresh supply every day.

That night, I slept in the treehouse. It was surprisingly comfortable, and I felt safe from the crabs. I slept soundly, dreaming about feasts of fresh fruit and fish.

* * * * *

The boy almost died today because of me. I feel terrible.

It rained in the morning, but Taly was hungry, so the boy and I went to the fishing spot. I hesitated to go out on the log because it was wet and slippery. The waves were rough, but the boy took the spear and confidently walked out. He dropped a coconut crumb in the water and waited.

I watched him through the rain from some nearby trees. Within a few minutes, he caught a small blue fish. He brought it to me, then returned to the log, and tossed in another crumb.

A minute later, he struck the water with his spear. He must have caught a bigger fish because the spear jerked and twisted in the boy's hands. He gripped it tightly, but the fish put up a fight. Suddenly, the spear jerked to the left, and the boy fell into the water.

The scene played out in slow motion for me. I saw the boy splashing and bobbing as he tried to keep his head above water. That's when I realized he didn't know how to swim. He was struggling to keep his head above the water, but he'd soon get tired from the effort. He was floating for now, but he wouldn't manage long in the rough water.

The boy would drown if I didn't help.

I froze. I was terrified that I'd fall in and that we'd both be in trouble. My swimming skills were suited to pools and calm water, not ocean waves.

Part of me told me that I had to help him, but part of me was frozen in fear. While I'd become stronger and more confident, I still couldn't conquer my fear of the water.

I knew I had to do something. I made my way across the log as quickly as I could. It was slippery, and a couple of times, I almost fell. I finally got to where he had fallen, but he was too far away. He was getting weaker and could barely stay afloat now. As I watched, his head sank beneath the water. He didn't come back up.

The spear floated nearby. I grabbed it and pushed it toward where the boy had gone under the water. Something bumped the spear under the water. I felt a weight on it. I pulled it up, felt the boy's hand on it, and grabbed it. The boy's head broke the surface. He gasped for air. I grabbed his hands, leaned back, and slowly pulled him onto the log. He sat gasping, but he was safe.

I was overwhelmed with relief but disappointed in myself. I was lucky to save him. He would have drowned if I'd waited any longer. I should have jumped in, but I just couldn't. It took every ounce of courage I had to come out on the log and reach out for him. The thought of jumping into the same ocean that had taken Dad away was unimaginable. I simply wasn't brave enough.

After the boy recovered, we brought the blue fish back to Taly. He ate it hungrily. I was happy to see that he looked much healthier and stronger than when I first met him.

* * * * *

The clouds cleared in the afternoon, and the sea became calm.

I found water in the bottle. The palm frond rainwater collection system had worked well. I took a sip of cool, fresh water. It was delicious and a welcome change from the coconut water.

As I drank, I felt a burning sensation on my thigh. I looked down to see a bright spot on my leg that moved as I moved the bottle. It took me a second to figure out where it came from. It was the bottle. The glass was acting like a lens for the sunlight, concentrating it into a bright spot.

I moved the bottle around in the sunlight, trying to make the spot as small as possible on the ground. The spot changed shape as I moved the bottle, but it didn't get any smaller. I tried the other bottles. I discovered that I could make a very bright spot with one of them if I turned it upside down with the bottom facing the sun. I touched the bright spot. It was hot!

I found a piece of dried coconut husk and used the bottle to aim the bright spot at the spongy interior. Nothing happened for a minute or so. Then I saw a wisp of smoke rise from the bright spot. The smoke grew. I blew on it. The pulp around the bright spot glowed red. A moment later, small flames flickered around the spot.

Fire! I smiled, feeling proud. I carried the husk to a clear spot in the clearing and added some husk pieces and sticks to build the flame. Before long, I had a roaring fire. Success!

I put the rest of the blue fish on a stick and cooked it over the fire. For the first time since I got to the island, I had cooked meat. It was delicious!

So now, I had food, water, a shelter, a light, and fire. I had gone from feeling terrified and helpless to feeling strong and confident. It felt good.

* * * * *

Today was a great day.

I had coconut meat and water for breakfast. By now, I was an expert at opening coconuts. I could lift the coconuts easily now, and I only needed two blows to open one—one to crack the husk and the other to crack the inner shell.

I also set up a stick in the clearing to help me track time. I stuck it vertically in the ground so it would cast a shadow throughout the day. I knew the shorter the shadow, the closer it was to noon. I placed a smaller stick where the shadow hit at noon and wrote *12* in the dirt beside it. I figured that should also be due north.

I started exercising. If I could be strong like the boy, I'd be in better shape to survive on the island. This morning, I ran along the beach and did push-ups and sit-ups. I planned to do this routine every morning. My body had already changed since I got here, becoming harder, stronger, and more muscular. I had more energy. My hair was longer, and my skin was deeply tanned.

That afternoon, I gathered more bananas. I used a long bamboo stalk to knock down the large green fruit nearby. It was hard and heavy. When I looked closely at it, its skin was dimpled with little hexagons. I remembered seeing a picture of one in class. It was a breadfruit.

I went fishing again and caught two fish. I gave the small one to Taly and saved the bigger one for my dinner.

That evening, I had the best meal yet on the island: warm cooked fish, roasted breadfruit (which tasted like potato), coconut water, and some bananas for dessert.

I walked to the beach. It was a beautiful sunset, so I stayed to watch it. On my way back to the tree, the stars came out. I used the trick Dad showed me to find the North Star. Sure enough, it was pretty much in line with my sundial stick.

I wrote my daily entry in the treehouse by the glow of my light bottle.

Wow, that was a great day, I thought as I lay down to sleep. A good breakfast, a way to track time and tell direction, exercise, enough food, a nice cooked dinner, a beautiful sunset, a treehouse to sleep in, and even light to write by.

Over the next few weeks, this became my routine: coconut for breakfast, exercise, fruit gathering, fish-catching, and dinner over a fire. I could get used to living like this.

I was building my strength and confidence. Every day, I felt stronger. It felt good.

* * * * *

One morning, I woke up before dawn and went to the east side
of the island to watch the sunrise. The ocean was as smooth as a mir-
ror, and the lightening sky was clear, except for some distant clouds
to the north. Slowly, the sky lightened to a soft pink. The sun rose a
few minutes later and flooded the air with light and warmth.

Taly was up and jumping around. It looked like his energy was
back, but he hadn't yet attempted to fly. I wonder if he didn't know
how or whether he was just happy staying with me, but something
didn't feel right about it. Birds should fly. I brought him up with me
to the treehouse, hoping to remind him of flight.

The boy sat on the branch. He stood up and swung down to the
ground. He looked expectantly at me. This time, I took a step down
the branch, leaned over, kicked off, and swung down beside him.
He looked at me, and I felt proud. He took off his necklace and put
it around my neck. I was honored. To me, the necklace was part of
him. I held the pendant in my hand. It was made from the branch of
a tree—our tree. It was a beautiful gift. I hugged him in appreciation.

I suddenly realized that he was no longer taller and bigger than
I was. We now stood eye to eye and shoulder to shoulder. It seemed
I'd grown in the past few weeks.

* * * *

It was another great day, with warm meals, time to exercise and play, and a beautiful sunset. The more I stayed on the island, the more I appreciated its beauty, from the warm beige of the big tree, the jewel green of the jungle, the deep blue of the water, and the bright yellows, reds, and blues of the fish. The pink, orange, and gold sunrises and sunsets were stunning, and the glittering stars along with the intense blue glow of the waves at night were so beautiful, it was like I was on another planet.

I began to think of the island as my own little playground. The treehouse was my house, the big tree was a jungle gym, and the beaches were sand pits, with shells as sand toys. Living on the island had become like playing every day.

But I knew I couldn't do this forever. I needed to rejoin my family. I needed to go to school, do my homework, and accept the other responsibilities I'd face as I grew older. I had to find a way back.

* * * * *

I heard fluttering when I woke up. It was Taly—he was flying! He flew to my hand as if to tell me something, and then he flew to the branch above.

I was delighted to see that he'd grown enough to fly. He was big and strong and confident now—far from the trembling baby I had first picked up. But part of me felt sad. He'd been my constant companion since I came to the island. I was worried that might change.

The branch I was on lifted me to reach him, but by the time I got there, he'd flown to the branch above me. We climbed above the canopy of palm trees to where the trunk narrowed, and there were no more branches to hold onto. Taly sat on the topmost branch. I held the trunk tightly.

We towered at least a hundred feet high over the jungle. The view from here was spectacular. I saw the entire island, the top of the jungle, and the surrounding beach. I saw my fishing log on the eastern side of the island. It was odd to see the island from this viewpoint. It looked like a miniature movie set. I realized how small and limited my world had become since I'd come to the island.

The surrounding ocean stretched into the horizon. It looked endless and enormous compared to my tiny island home. I realized how isolated I truly was.

I looked at Taly, and he looked at me. Then, without warning, he jumped off the branch and started flying. He flew well, both wings strongly beating. He turned north and flew over the palm trees, over the shoreline, over the ocean, and toward the clouds I'd seen to the north earlier. I watched him until he was a tiny speck in the sky, and just like that, he was gone. My loyal companion had recovered and flown away.

Where did he go? I wondered. Why did he head toward those clouds?

That's when it hit me. Those clouds were always on the northern horizon every time I looked. That was unusual. Clouds didn't stay in one place. So why were these clouds always in the same place?

Land—I remember seeing clouds motionless over Maui and the other Hawaiian islands.

I felt a sudden shift. I gripped the trunk more tightly. All this time, the island drifted in its own little universe far away from the rest of the world. I knew that I had to find a way to get back to the real world and to my home, but I never had a specific idea where that might be.

But now, I had a glimpse of where the way back home might be—to the north.

I knew it wasn't Enedrik. Enedrik wasn't large enough to hold clouds. Based on the prevailing winds and where I washed up, I probably came from the south. Going back to Enedrik would be difficult. It was small, and I'd have to travel against the wind. It would be too easy to miss, and the last thing I wanted was to end up in the open ocean.

My hopes lay to the north.

Something had changed in the space of a few moments. I knew this shift meant that my life was about to change forever. As soon as I saw the land to the north, I knew I had to try and reach it, even though it wouldn't be easy. My future was waiting on that land to the north.

I knew that my carefree time on the island was coming to an end.

* * * * *

I woke up at the first light of dawn and started building my boat the next day.

In retrospect, it was obvious that I needed to build a boat. What other way was there off the island? I wasn't sure why I hadn't started this already.

But I had not. Maybe I was too young and scared and too dependent on others to help me. Maybe I never really had accepted my situation. Maybe I had never really taken responsibility for solving the problem or had the confidence to believe I could. Maybe I never really believed there *was* other land out there until I had seen it. Maybe I could never even imagine overcoming my terror of the ocean and being brave enough to set out on it again.

But now, things were different. I knew land was out there. It was time to accept that only I could resolve my situation. I knew I could do it. I was physically and mentally stronger and more mature now. Somewhere to the north was another place, a way to get home. And while I was still terrified of the ocean, I knew it was time to face that fear. For the first time, I felt ready to try.

The boy helped. He always seemed to appear when I needed him. We started by making rope from vines. We pulled down long vines from the trees and trimmed off the leaves. Then we braided three vines together to make a strong rope and braided three of those braided vines together to make an even stronger rope. I knew from our experience with the treehouse that the vines would dry out and lose their strength after about a week. I hoped I wouldn't need them for longer.

We went through the jungle, gathering logs to build the boat frame. We needed four for the four sides and one to set diagonally to make a closed Z. We tied all the joints tightly together with the strong rope. Then we placed a bamboo platform on top of the frame like the one we used for the treehouse.

For extra flotation, we gathered a bunch of older, lighter coconuts and placed them under the platform between the frame logs. We finished the base by adding a second floor beneath the logs to secure the coconuts and keep them in place. We also found some driftwood to use as oars, which we secured on either side with strips of rope.

It looked seaworthy, but it was more of a floating platform than a boat. Because it looked like it could wander in any direction, I called it the Wanderer.

We finished the boat by dinner time. It lay on the beach, small in size but big in hope. The boat was my way out, my way back to my real life, whatever that was. I looked at it in awe, fear, and hope.

The boy and I enjoyed a tasty dinner of fish, coconut, banana, and roasted breadfruit under the tree. We stayed up late, gazing at the stars until I finally drifted off to sleep. I dreamed of boats and strange new lands.

* * * * *

It didn't work.

I woke up excited to try out the Wanderer. It was a beautiful sunny day, and the winds were just right. *A perfect day for a boat ride*, I thought.

I was scared but excited. Now that I chose to leave the island, now that the boat was a reality, I was anxious and eager to go. While the island had become my home instead of a frightening place, I knew I was destined for somewhere else.

After my morning exercise, I pushed the Wanderer to the edge of the water. A wave broke beneath and lifted it. It floated! Energized, I pushed it out as quickly as I could onto the water and hopped onto it. I grabbed the oars and started paddling from shore.

So far, so good. The boat floated quite well, and I found I could make headway with the paddle.

When the first wave hit, the boat leaned over so much, I had to grab the edge to keep from falling off. It stayed upright, but now, I was paddling sideways to the waves. I tried to turn into the next wave, but it hit before I was ready.

I felt the boat tip sharply until I slid into the water. I tasted salt water, and my eyes stung. I shot upright. Fortunately, the water was still shallow enough for me to stand with my head above the water. I stood there for a moment, coughing and sputtering until I got my breath back. I looked behind me and saw the Wanderer flipped upside down. I grabbed it and pulled it ashore.

The good news was that the boat held together and floated. The bad news was it was unstable. If I had any hopes of reaching the land to the north, I had to find a way to keep it from flipping in the surf.

* * * * *

I woke up early and made breakfast, but it wasn't the same without Taly. It was too quiet, too still. I already missed my friend and realized how much his companionship meant to me.

After breakfast, I thought about how to make the boat more stable. I remembered from my reading that Polynesians took small boats on the ocean. They used logs attached to one or both sides of their canoes, or outriggers, to stabilize them. Maybe that's what I needed.

I found two logs about the right length and two bamboo stalks and attached them to the Wanderer so that each log was a couple of feet away from the main section. I tied everything tightly with braided vines. It certainly looked more stable. I also added a short mast to attach supplies and use as a crude sundial and way to see if I was headed north.

I took the boat out to the water again. This time, it worked much better. The boat still leaned when it crested the waves, but it never felt like it would tip over. When I passed the breaking surf and the seas were calmer, the boat was much more stable. I even discovered that the outriggers helped keep the boat moving in a straight path. Success!

Something clicked in me. I was really going to do this. I was going to leave the island.

I spent the rest of the day gathering supplies for the trip. I was guessing the horizon, as seen from the top of the tree, was about 20 miles away based on what I remembered from old whaling stories. This was assuming the top of the tree was similar in height to a crow's nest on a whaling ship. I knew I couldn't paddle very fast, maybe 1 mile per hour during daylight hours, so I'd have to plan to be at sea for at least two days. Just to be safe, I packed for five.

That afternoon, I went fishing and caught six large fish. I roasted them and three breadfruit over a fire. I ate one fish for dinner and wrapped the rest in palm leaves. I put them in my treehouse along with the roasted breadfruit. Then I gathered some vines and made a net to carry supplies.

That night, I dreamed of paddling across the ocean and coming ashore at Alki Beach. My family was there to greet me. I saw my home on the hill and the Space Needle across the bay.

* * * * *

Today marked a momentous occasion—the day I bid farewell
to the island that had been my home for so long. The morning was
consumed by the meticulous task of packing. The net brimmed with
freshly caught fish, ripe breadfruit, a bunch of bananas, and a collection of five unbroken coconuts, carefully chosen for their precious
water content, while an equal number of broken coconuts were set
aside for sustenance. My cherished journal and pens found refuge
within a plastic bag, safeguarding them from moisture. I had devised
a plan to use one of the pens to bore holes in the coconuts for drinking purposes, securing the bag firmly to the mast to prevent any
mishaps.

With everything stowed away, I stood by the boat and cast a lin-
gering gaze back at the island. By now, every nook and cranny of the
place was etched in my memory: the sandy shores, the lush jungle,
my favorite fishing spot, the serene clearing, and the towering tree
that had been my constant companion. It had become so intimately
familiar that it felt like an intrinsic part of myself. Departing from
the island was akin to leaving behind a version of my own identity.
The island had transformed me—I had arrived as a frightened young
boy, and now, I was departing as a self-assured young man, forever
shaped by my time here. The memories would stay with me eternally.

I made my way to the clearing for one last poignant look at my
island sanctuary, brimming with recollections of my life here. The
remnants of palm fronds, which had served as my initial shelter, still
lay in a heap. Coconut husks were scattered about, evidence of the
sustenance that had sustained me. My hand-crafted Bionicles were
strewn haphazardly across the ground. The fire pit, surrounded by

empty bottles, bore testimony to countless evenings spent under the starry sky. And then there was my treehouse, nestled in the arms of the tree that had been my protector throughout my stay. Everything seemed smaller now—the palm trees, the clearing, and the tree itself. I approached the tree and tenderly embraced its trunk one final time.

As I returned to the boat, a pang of realization struck me—I hadn't seen the boy in a few days. To be honest, my focus had been consumed by the urgency of my departure, and the thought of him had slipped my mind. Nevertheless, it felt incomplete to leave the island without bidding him farewell. My gaze shifted upward, and there he stood, observing me from the edge of the jungle.

* * * *

We locked eyes for a full minute, an unusual pause in our inter-actions. Until that moment, it hadn't even crossed my mind to con-sider taking him along. As far as I knew, this island was his world, the only home he'd ever known, and the place he'd always call his own. To me, he was an inseparable part of this island's essence, and the thought of him anywhere else seemed inconceivable.

However, the moment I glimpsed his expression, my heart soft-ened, and I realized I couldn't leave without him. I retraced my steps, reached out, and took his hand, silently conveying my intentions. Together, we made our way back to the boat. A smile graced his lips, but no words passed between us. Side by side, we pushed the boat into the water until it began to float. With nimble coordination, we climbed aboard, each of us grabbing an oar, ready to navigate the uncertain waters ahead. Safely, we cleared the tumultuous surf that threatened our departure.

Certain life experiences possess the power to profoundly trans-form a person, serving as a bridge between one chapter of life and the next. I was acutely aware that my time on the island was one such experience. Here, I had learned, evolved, and grown in ways I couldn't have imagined. What had started with my arrival as a timid, frightened boy was culminating in my departure as a self-assured young man. As much as a part of me wished to linger in this haven, I recognized it was time to depart. I needed to reunite with my family, resume my education, and begin contemplating college and the path that lay beyond. It was time to rejoin the world beyond the island's shores and find my place in the realm of reality.

Our combined weight gently pressed the boat lower into the water, creating a noticeable but reassuring stability. Yet the act of paddling proved more strenuous than I had anticipated. We had to lean out precariously and exert ourselves against the water's resistance. The boat rode the waves, sometimes delving too deeply, at other times skimming the surface. Gradually, we established a rhythm, propelling ourselves forward through our synchronized efforts.

Heading northward along the island's eastern shoreline, we ventured further into the open sea. The character of the waves transformed as we distanced ourselves from the familiarity of the island— evolving from short choppy surges to long rolling undulations. The water grew darker and colder, and the boat settled into a steady, reassuring rocking motion as our paddles sliced through the deepening waters.

* * * * *

We synchronized our movements with each stroke of the paddle, plunging it into the sea, propelling the water behind us, and then repeating the motion. The boy and I maintained this rhythm throughout the morning, occasionally switching sides to grant our arms some much-needed respite. At one point, I dared to cast a backward glance. The island was quickly retreating. I watched as it gradually receded, dissolving into the vast expanse of unbroken ocean, a fading memory of my past.

Surrounded by the deep dark waters, the effort of paddling relentlessly began to take its toll. Sweat trickled down my skin as I labored at the oars, prompting me to remove my shirt and tie it securely to the mast. A quick glance at the boy revealed a startling resemblance between us now. With my shirt off, my weather-beaten shorts, long hair, and sun-kissed skin, we bore such a striking similarity that one could easily mistake us for twins.

As midday approached, our navigation became increasingly challenging. The absence of the island as a reference point, combined with the sun directly overhead, left us disoriented. On the distant horizon, a couple of cloud banks loomed, and I couldn't discern which one to paddle toward. We decided to take a break to rest and have lunch—a meal of freshly caught fish complemented by coconut. I was surprised by the intensity of my hunger and, more notably, my thirst. Paddling demanded far more energy than I had anticipated. I drained the water from a whole coconut, yet my thirst persisted.

Surveying the seemingly infinite expanse of ocean around us, memories of the night I lost my dad rushed back to me. Although the weather was bright and calm now, it still felt as though we were riding atop the back of an immense slumbering beast. I could sense its salty breath and feel the briny moisture as the waves splashed against the boat's sides. It inhaled deeply with each rolling wave, stretching to the horizon in every direction—a colossal creature of boundless size and power. It lay dormant at the moment, but I couldn't shake the awareness that it could awaken with unimaginable fury at any instant. A shiver ran down my spine.

After some time, the sun had shifted enough to give us a rough sense of direction again. Judging by the trajectory of the early afternoon sun, I chose one of the cloud banks as our new course. Yet the further we paddled into the open ocean, the more uneasy I became. Doubts about the wisdom of embarking on such a voyage in our small makeshift boat gnawed at me. What if the sea beast awakened? What if there was no land beneath those clouds? I cast another glance at the boy, who displayed no fear, and found the resolve to press on. We continued to paddle, driven by an unspoken determination.

*　*　*　*

Later that afternoon, as the boy and I switched positions at the oars, I couldn't help but notice a peculiar disturbance in the water behind us—a looming, solitary swell trailing our tiny boat. Perplexed, I leaned over the boat's stern, squinting against the sun's glare to get a better look. And then I saw it: a face beneath the water's surface. A colossal, nightmarish countenance adorned with rows of razor-sharp teeth and obsidian eyes fixed upon me. There was no mistaking it; it was a shark, a monstrous leviathan dwarfing our humble vessel.

It stared at me, its unblinking gaze locking onto mine. Merely a few feet away and barely visible beneath the waves, its massive head swayed rhythmically as it tracked our movements. Panic gnawed at the edges of my thoughts. I understood all too well that it could attack without warning, and a shark of that magnitude had the power to shred our boat to pieces. The futility of attempting to fend it off with our oars in the event of an assault only added to my sense of vulnerability. We were adrift in the vastness of the ocean, entirely at its mercy.

The fear that coursed through me now was different from the paralyzing dread I'd experienced during the storm that took my father from me. This was a visceral terror, born of imminent danger and the stark realization of our helplessness. A sobering thought crossed my mind—had we erred in leaving the island? While remaining would have meant forfeiting any chance of reuniting with my family or experiencing the world beyond, at least the boy and I would have been safe.

But there was no retreat; there was only the ceaseless rhythm of our paddles against the water. I had to confront my fear and press forward. I kept a vigilant eye on the shark as we forged ahead, noting its reluctance to draw nearer, as if it were pondering its next move.

After what felt like an interminable stretch of time, the shark abruptly swiveled its tail and vanished into the ocean's depths. I continued to watch, apprehensive, but it never resurfaced. With a protracted, shuddering breath, I released the grip of fear that had clung to me. For now, the sea had spared us its savage fury.

* * * * *

The world has indeed grown smaller in the past century. What were once arduous voyages spanning months can now be completed comfortably within hours aboard a modern plane. Distant lands and cultures have been brought closer, accessible through the swift dissemination of news and social media. Personal communication has transcended time and space, happening instantaneously.

However, beneath this veneer of connectivity lies the immutable truth that our world remains profoundly immense. Nowhere is this more apparent than from the perspective of a diminutive boat, gently bobbing on the boundless open sea. Waves extended as far as our eyes could discern, stretching out in every conceivable direction. And our tiny circle of visibility was but a minuscule fraction of the vastness that surrounded us.

We continued paddling until the sun dipped below the horizon, painting the sky with hues of twilight just before the stars emerged. It was time for another respite, this one under the celestial canopy. Our dinner consisted of freshly caught fish, breadfruit, and coconut meat, complemented by sips of the precious water we had brought along. Concern gnawed at me as I watched our water supply dwindle rapidly. Between the relentless heat and the exertion of paddling, we were consuming it at a faster rate than anticipated. In less than a day, three of the five water coconuts were already depleted.

With the moon ascending and casting its radiant glow upon the ocean, we used the North Star as our guiding light, resuming our journey with synchronized strokes. By now, we had become so attuned to each other's movements that we moved in perfect harmony, our oars slicing through the water in unison. We paddled for hours, shifting from one side to the other at regular intervals.

Even though the water was relatively calm, the sight of the dark rolling waves stirred unsettling memories from my nightmares. After several hours of paddling, we decided to halt for the night. I found myself instinctively gripping the mast as I drifted into sleep, haunted by haunting visions reminiscent of my troubled dreams.

* * * * *

In the morning, an impenetrable shroud of dense fog enveloped us. It was so thick that our vision extended no farther than a few feet in any direction. Within this eerie cocoon, our boat and the small patch of ocean surrounding it seemed to constitute a world unto themselves, isolated from the realm of reality.

Hours passed as we patiently waited for a change in the weather, but the fog clung to us relentlessly, refusing to yield even the slightest hint of a clearer path. With only one water coconut remaining, our situation had grown dire. We could no longer afford to drift aimlessly. Somehow, we needed to muster the strength to paddle toward land, although we were entirely ignorant of its whereabouts.

Until this point, we had always relied on guiding factors—the sun, the stars, a rudimentary sundial or compass, and sometimes even the presence of clouds on the horizon or the sight of the receding island behind us. But now, there was nothing but an impenetrable white curtain obscuring our surroundings. The question gnawed at me: How could I possibly discern the correct direction to navigate? The stakes were too high to allow room for mistakes.

A surge of panic welled up within me, urging me to take action, to start paddling in any direction. Yet another part of me recognized the peril in such impulsivity. Haphazard paddling might lead us in circles or further away from our salvation. "Think!" I admonished myself. "How can I ascertain the direction to land?"

Lying down on the platform of the boat, I pondered our predicament as it gently rocked beneath me. The rhythmic sound of waves crashing against the hull echoed in my ears—*slap-slap, slap-slap*.

"Slap-slap," I repeatedly said to myself, finding the pattern peculiar.

In my expectation, waves should have maintained a steady rhythm—*slap, slap, slap*. However, what I observed were waves arriving in pairs, like a synchronized dance. My focus sharpened as I scrutinized the waves around us. Initially, they appeared as a chaotic jumble, devoid of any discernible pattern. But after a few moments, I discerned two superimposed sets of waves. The primary waves rolled from nearly directly behind us, but a second significantly smaller set emanated from ahead and slightly to our right. It was the interplay of these two wave sets that produced the curious slapping rhythm against the boat.

"Why would there be two sets of waves?" I wondered aloud, the realization dawning upon me. I had witnessed this phenomenon before—in my childhood bathtub. When I pushed water toward the side of the tub, it resulted in waves that collided with the wall, but subsequently, a secondary smaller set of waves rebounded.

"That's it!" I exclaimed silently. "The second set of waves must be reflected from land! Land is ahead and to our right."

In other circumstances, I might have hesitated, waiting for more evidence or seeking confirmation from others. However, this was not one of those times. The responsibility rested squarely on my shoulders and mine alone.

With newfound determination, the boy and I began paddling toward the source of the secondary waves. The sky grew darker, and a few hours later, the fog lifted, revealing the starry expanse above. Our course had held true north, just as I had hoped. A sense of pride welled up within me.

* * * * *

The total darkness of Enedrik enveloped us like a shroud, plunging us into a void deeper than the abyss. Unlike the familiar glow of my hometown, where streetlights and headlights painted feeble streaks of light, or even the distant city's glow on the horizon, this remote realm offered no such comforts. Here, the air and water melded into an inky blackness so profound that it felt as if my eyelids were forever sealed.

We pressed on through the night, our relentless paddling matched only by the relentless ache of our parched throats. In this suffocating obscurity, the urgency of reaching land pressed down upon us. Yet, within this obsidian abyss, the distance to salvation remained inscrutable. We might be a mere mile from shore, or the land we sought could lie a merciless fifty miles distant. Doubt crept into my thoughts, and I began to question whether we would ever emerge from this Stygian void.

A few hours after the fog's dissipating act, the winds stirred with increasing ferocity, their mournful howls tugging at our clothing and our resolve. A tempest of anxiety swirled within my stomach.

The boy, however, appeared impervious to the changing weather. With every rhythmic stroke of his paddle, he propelled us forward, our combined efforts aimed at wrestling control from the encroaching fury of the waves. I mirrored his resilience, summoning every ounce of strength to navigate through the surging surf and the mounting gales.

Later in the night, a full-blown storm descended upon us, casting us into a maelstrom of even more formidable winds and towering waves. Glimpses of starlight punctuated gaps in the shrouding clouds, revealing whitecaps swirling malevolently around us. Raindrops lashed at my face, and the waves swelled in stature, some rising above us like ancient titans surging forth. The sea had metamorphosed into an unrelenting adversary, rendering our continued paddling an exercise in futility. Huddled within the boat, we clung tenaciously to its sides and mast as it bucked and reeled beneath us. The shocking degradation of our situation left me immobilized, while fear regained its suffocating grip.

As the night advanced, the wind and waves coalesced into a gargantuan howling beast, toying with our precarious vessel. It pitched and rolled with a ferocity that demanded every ounce of our strength to maintain our tenuous grip.

In my mind's eye, images from my nightmares flickered vividly. Save for the boy's presence and the makeshift boat, this was the very embodiment of those harrowing dreams. Monstrous waves thundered toward us like freight trains hurtling through the dark void. Shivering in the ceaseless onslaught of rain and wind, I wrestled with paralyzing terror, striving to wrest control from its stranglehold and focus on our dire predicament.

Then, in a moment of profound disbelief, an enormous wave surged over us, leaving us desperately clinging to our boat for dear life. Blinking away the freezing deluge, I realized our oars were gone, torn from our grasp by the relentless sea.

Another wave descended with a deafening crash, drenching us anew, and our net gave way, flinging our precious cargo of fish and coconuts into the unfathomable depths of the inky abyss. We clung resolutely to the boat as it twisted and tumbled perilously.

Crash! A behemoth of a wave swallowed us whole, breaking off the outriggers and subjecting the boat to an unrelenting series of somersaults. I clung tenaciously to the vessel, summoning every last vestige of strength, miraculously remaining aboard as it righted itself.

Yet the boy was gone, and my heart plummeted into a chasm of despair. Fear engulfed me as I frantically scanned the tempestuous waters, spotting him some ten feet away, his struggle for survival painted against the canvas of the relentless sea.

I knew his strength was fleeting, that the ruthless currents threatened to rend us asunder, and that he would succumb without my intervention. I also knew that my only sanctuary lay within the precarious shelter of our battered boat.

In life, there exist moments when rational deliberation is a luxury denied, when decisions cannot abide contemplation—in such moments, action becomes the sole imperative, fear be damned.

I rose from my position, took two resolute steps toward the boy, and hurled myself into the maelstrom's churning heart.

EPILOGUE

My saviors would recount the day they chanced upon me, washed ashore upon a desolate beach, our battered vessel's remnants strewn nearby. I stood, a sunburnt, parched, and half-delirious semblance of my former self, a mere specter of who I had once been. With an urgency born of compassion, they carried me to the hospital, with my incessant queries about the boy I had saved, the one who had washed ashore alongside me, leaving them bewildered. His enigmatic disappearance mirrored his enigmatic arrival, an enigma that still haunts my thoughts, leading me to contemplate whether he arrived as my guardian angel.

A decade and a half have elapsed since I bade farewell to that island. Even as I've blossomed into an independent adult, leading a self-reliant life, recollections of that place and the boy persistently cast their enduring shadows whenever I close my eyes. In the sanctuary of my mind's eye, I still behold Taly, my chirping and hopping companion, and the towering guardian tree that once shielded me. I revisit the enchanting dawns and dusks, the delicate seashells gracing the shoreline, the stars crafting a tapestry in the night sky with their shimmering brilliance, and the ethereal blue glow of the bioluminescent waves.

The island was more than just a chapter in the story of my life; it was my rite of passage, an indelible fragment of my cherished childhood that, alas, could not withstand the relentless march of time. Among the most profound lessons etched into my soul by that island was the essence of bravery. It unveiled to me that courage isn't the absence of fear but rather the art of mastering fear and forging ahead despite its tenacious grip. Today, I confront most of my fears with newfound fortitude, and when doubt looms large, I simply reach beneath my shirt to touch the pendant that serves as my guiding talisman.

ABOUT THE AUTHOR

Brian Conte is a technologist and proud father of three kids. This is his first story. He spent three weeks on a desert island with his son, Zeb, who was the inspiration for this story.